BUILD
UNIVERSES

Jason Ó Fionnáin

GODS & FIGHTING MEN
~ The Secret Union ~

europe books

© 2020 **Europe Books**| London
www.europebooks.co.uk | info@europebooks.co.uk

ISBN   9791220110792
First edition: December 2020

GODS & FIGHTING MEN
The Secret Union

I wish to quote from Lady Gregory's 1905 book:

"We would not give up our own Country—Ireland—if we were to get the whole world as an estate, and the Country of the Young along with it."

I wish to acknowledge and confirm that if it was not for the knowledge I am privileged to have received through the original writings of Lady Gregory, W.B. Yeats, The Book of Invasions and the years of Irish folklore and tales in my youth and if notfor them, my work on the film project and this the first book, episode one would not see the light of day.

I acknowledge that my original script and version of the story of Fionn, The Tuatha dé Danann and theFianna of Ireland is my original thought and work.
My research for the past five years has given me great knowledge and insight into our great and wonderful history and my very own heritage, as well as giving me an understanding of life itself.

THE GOLDEN AGE RETURNS

Preface

It was May 1st 2018 known as Beltane when I made a short trip with my wife and youngest son of three across the hidden heartlands of county Westmeath to a very special place called Uisneach, the sacred center of Ireland were our sovereign goddess and queen Ériu of The Tuatha dé Danann rests beneath the stone of divisions. Uisneach was once the capital center of Mide, the fifth province of Eire. It was also the place of royal meetings, ceremonies and festivals.

It was a short 27-minute drive I had meant to do for years but always missed it for some reason or another. The date was important to me as I had to visit during the time known as Beltane.

As we walked around the site and land it gave me a feeling of calm, a feeling of true freedom that I belonged and that I was safe from all harm in the world. When we got to the top of the hill I could see the whole of Ireland, North, South, West and East with the Sun and Moon balancing my view. It was breath-taking in the most meaningful way, I mean it made me feel likeI was home.

Our guide on that day was local archaeologist and storyteller Justin, whom I know from our local nuts and grains store, the place where we get our natural goodies.

As he told us his stories under the ancient Hawthorn, beside the long grass of Lough Lugh, stories of the Tuatha dé and the invasions of Ireland I felt I heard them all before and under- stood and by some strange connection I felt that I could finish each of the stories as if I wrote them myself.

My research in the years previous to my visit had obviously increased my knowledge, but it was more than that, in this place it was almost like I had been their many times before.

For years I planned to visit Uisneach for inspiration for the film project I was working on but I had no idea the effect it would have over me, especially when we made our way down the valley to the resting place of Ériu. The power of the stone and energy around it was clearly present on the second day I visited with local tour guide and musician storyteller Marty, I crawled under the stone from one side to the other.

It was truly a surreal moment in time as I went in on my knees and turned inside to come out on my back with the help from friends as they pulled me out by my arms as if to be reborn and blessed by Ériu herself.

I went back a third time for the famous festival of fires in 2019 as a witness to the ancient tradition, the beacon of communication and light in the darkness among the other gatherings at peaks around the four corners of Ireland was amazing. On my forth visit with some cast and crew for the film project I left with a feeling of excitement and drive. I wanted to go for it now and begin filming the project, but I had one more trip to make before I could start.

It was another journey I had put on the long finger, a distant drive this time to the coast of County Cork near the river blackwater, Youghal.

It is there when I finally caught up with an old friend I had not seen for ten years, "Draoi" Cathy Coyle who was helping me take a different kind of journey.

The journey was quite different from any other I have ever taken. It was a journey of healing Insight and a unique path-way to my Gaelic lineage.
I would probably never be able to fully describe the experience and if I tried you would think I was mad or a few screws loose as they say but I can say it was very real and over two hours of transcendence that took me from my childhood all the way through every main event and emotion to present and future.

I physically felt the force and divine power in my hands and chest as I continued to deeply inhale and exhale.

I will never forget it for as long as I live and Cathy is a true Draoi. She has a gift of our ancient heritage and she told me afterwards that we had twelve visitors around us that day, witnessing my experience as I opened my soul for reading. Those figures present were the spirits of The Tuatha dé and if I was to take anything from it afterwards, and even now as I write these words, they were making sure I was worthy of the task ahead, the right person for the quest I had taken on.

I may never know the real reason for their presence but I am honoured and privileged they bother with me and since then I have been gifted sign after signs of help as I continue moving forward on this journey of life and to share these ancient stories the best way I can.

Dedication

I dedicate this book to the brave fighting men and women whofought and sacrificed their lives through the age of Pisces against foreign invaders with envious eyes and greed and destruction of our precious way of life, who attempted to remove the children and decadence of this island without success so that we now rise from a buried and shackled past with a new uncontrolled clear vision as a united brothers and sisters of Éireann.

Introduction

According to Legend, The Tuatha dé Danann were a mystical race of God-like beings who came and ruled around five thousand years ago. Modern day scholars deny they ever existed, yet ancient storytellers have left behind many clues including DNA, text and carvings of the most incredible finds and passed down the wonderful stories about them and the Bloodlinethey left behind.

Table of Contents

Series One
~ **The Fianna** ~

Episode One
~ **The Secret Union** ~

Chapter One
~ **Muirne and Cumhaill** ~

or now is the Age of Pisces, a time of surrender, compassion, empathy and sacrifice. A time when warriors transcended into Saints and Scholars.

The symbol of Christianity is strong in Europe and beginning to make its way and take hold in Éireann, changing the ancient ways and beliefs of the Gaelic people of Danu & Éireann.

In the year 173 AD, Ireland flourished in a golden age of Kings & Queens, Scholars & Poets, Warriors and Druids.
The island was divided into five provinces, Ulster, Munster, Leinster, Connacht & Mide. Each province was ruled by a King &Queen with one High King chosen to rule all the land.

The High King at that time was chosen by the third of four gifts from the Gods, The Lia Fáil, The Stone of Destiny kept at The Hill of Tara where Conn Cétchathach of a Hundred Battles was coroneted. A true High King after hundreds of years, and where it was said that not since therage of
Cú Chulainn did the stone cry out.

Conn's greatest soldier, protector and Captain of Clan Baiscne, Rígfhéinnid leader and chieftain of Fianna Ná Éireann, The Fianna of Ireland, He was the warrior known as Cumhaill Mac Trenmór.

Cumhaill was a great warrior like his father before him and came from a long line of fighting men famously known as the sons of Trenmór.

He served as a protector of Ireland since boyhood and was loyal to Conn and a favorite of Queen Eithne.

Cumhaill was no longer a young man and felt it was time to settle down and wed and have a son of his own. He had many opportunities in his life but only one turned his head, only one did his heart belong too.

Her name was Muirne Muncháem with the beautiful long neck, andshe was on her father's line, a descendant of The Tuatha dé Danann, the ancient Neolithic living gods of Ireland.

Muirne's father was the great Druid Tadg Mac Nuadat and he wasthe direct grandchild of the Great Nuada, first King of The Tuatha dé Danann.

Tadg was Conn's advisory aide and the King understood the oldways very well, even though he was not of the lineage.

Tadg wanted Muirne to marry a King or a man of the Tuatha dé bloodline. He warned the King of a prophecy that would change everything if this did not happen.

Tadg did not know about the secret love between Muirne and Cumhaill.

When the secret became a gossip whisper and the druid Tadg heard of this talk, he was furious and asked the King for the first time to end Cumhaill.

Conn refused his request and said, "Cumhaill will not betray me and the prophecy is not true Tadg, you are mistaken."

"I will send Cumhaill on a mission" he said, to retrieve the stolen Spear of Lugh ('sleá bua') The Spear of Victory, the second gift from the gods."

"Will this make you happy?" Conn asked a very unhappy Tadg as he paced back and forth across the floors of the Brú na Bóinne.

Tadg stops and replies, "This will be the end of life as we know it, I will not forgive this and the sea will take him if I have anything to do with it, I forbid the union of my daughter with Cumhaill mac Trenmór."

Tadg stormed out and the King was saddened by the news. He nowmust send Cumhaill away and while he goes to sit to write his mission quest, he noticed a crow fly out of the palace window.

Before Tadg leaves Tara, he speaks with a member of The Fianna known as Aedh Mac Morna of The Morna clan of Connacht, one half of The Fianna.

Aedh was a young determent warrior who, along with his brothers, also came from a long line of fighting men, who were always envious of Cumhaill, and while Captain of Clan Morna hewanted to be Leader of the Fianna and overthrow Cumhaill from his position. But Cumhaill is stronger and wiser and number one to the King and Queen.

As Tadg passed Aedh, Aedh asked, "Can I speak with you Tadg?"Tadg didn't answer him and continued to leave. Aedh said again, "I'm at your service if ever you need me?"

Tadg looked back and stamped his staff three times in the dirt then pulled over his hood saying, "We will speak again Aedh Mac Morna".
He then turned and went on his way.

Aedh shook his head in disappointment saying, "Crazy old Druid". Aedh then made his way into the King.

The Crow that flew out of the palace was no ordinary bird. His name was Fiachra and he was the companion to Cumhaill's druidess sister Bodhmall.

Bodhmall often sent Fiachra on spy missions to help her brother in the past, but since she left the homestead to live in the wild forests and mountain caves of Éireann, she only returns when needed.

Draoí Bodhmall is a farsighted prophetic woman of nature who devotes her life to ancient ways of The Tuatha dé Danann and the survival instincts of her Gaelic ancestors. One of her many skills are to see and hear through the creatures she lives among nature.

Bodhmall awaited in her mountain cave for word, and when she received the news through Fiachra about her brother's secret affair with the High Druid's daughter and close friend no longer a secret and that he was being sent away on a dangerous mission to the war-torn Roman province of Gallia.

she felt ill with a vision of him in grave life-threatening danger.

Bodhmall called out in prayer through the Ogham travel door   for divine help and guidance.

That same night The Goddess queen Mórrígan of The Tuatha dé intervened by making three visits.

The first was Bodhmall, telling her what needs to be done for the prophecy, meaning she would need to immediately make her way toward the family homestead.

The second was to Muirne, warning her of how little time she had to prepare for what was to come.

The third visit standing over him was to a sleeping Cumhaill Mac Trenmór, who, like the many great warriors before him she was very fond of, the prophecy she told him and what lay ahead and that it was he who must see her signs and listen and understand her guidance for she is there in the darkness with him and those who are strong and wise and willing to choose path of severance.

"Cumhaill Mac Trenmór" she called in her sure and whispering voice as she moved around his resting place, "you must go to the secret stones and bind with Muirne Muncháem and lay with her, for you will be gifted and blessed with a child who will unite all against foreign invasion. He will be a great warrior and leader like you, and one day a King and protector of our lands.
You must then go on a quest for the lost Sleá Bua 'spear of Lugh' and you must bring it home."

Cumhaill awoke to the sound of a crow and stepped outside, looking upon the full moonlight with the arms of autumn trees holding in the night blue sky. It was at that moment that he understood his purpose in life.

As the crow passed through his line of sight, Cumhaill speaks out, "I hear you my lady, goddess of night and I give you my word, my strength and my honour and I am graciously thankful for your guidance."

The reply of one caw he hears in the distance as the crow flies down to the black silhouette of trees.
The following day Cumhaill meets with his King and receives his mission request and well wishes for his journey with a blessing from the Queen.

Normally for occasions such of high importance, the High Druid would bless the warrior but Tadg was nowhere to be seen.

Cumhaill did not stay long and told the King before he left, "I will not let you down my King, I will return with Lúin".

The King replied with a saddened smile, "I am knowing you will, son of Trenmór".

Cumahill on his beautiful horse companion Raithneach Mhuire (Lady Fern) galloped away like a young man once again.

***

As the evening mystic fog fell over the sun setting valley of the sacred stone circle near the Trenmór homestead, Bodhmall appears from the forest on foot alongside the mist blanket covered pond with her staff and trappings.

The air was different from any other time in this place and the sense of sadness was in her for her brother and dear friend as they will celebrate alone with no others.

The crow of Mórrígan from a branch above called out three times as Bodhmall enters the 12 strong standing stone circle where the ancient spirits of the past are present and watching.

This was a witnessed milestone of marriage between a bloodlineto The Tuatha dé in Murine Muncháem and bloodline to The Gaelin Cumhaill Mac Trenmór.

Bodhmall waits in the midst and from Ailm (the West) Muirne arrives, and at the same time from hÚath (the East) Cumhaill arrives, both holding a gift for each other.
Cumhaill's gift is a triple braided bronze torc and Muirne hasa matching bracelet for her loving warrior.

She looks at him as she steps into the circle from behind thetall Ailm stone and smiles at him as they walk toward Bodhmallat the middle.

Cumhaill gently places the torc around the beautiful long neck of Muirne, and she looks at him with clear glass hazel & green coloured eyes.

Muirne takes Cumhaill's arm and places the bracket upon it. He smiles at her while holding her hand as a gesture of calm to indicate that all will be as it should be. She reacts with a smile by holding his other wrist as they prepare to be joined.Bodhmall takes the bark tray, of Celtic Woad made from the specially chosen the Isatis tinctorial plant from the flat laying Center stone.

She places the blessed blue green paint to the foreheads of Muirne and Cumhaill. She then takes three binding ropes and places over theirholding hands.

She then sprinkles a hand full of soil over the ropes saying the words:

"Bennacht tire" (Blessing of Earth).

She wraps ropes around the wrists of Muirne and Cumhaill, a second time with a knot, and spills from a wooden bowl water over the knot saying, "Bennacht Mara" (Blessing of Sea). She wraps the ropes around again tying a third knot and by gliding her hand through the warm wind over them and placing the air upon the knots and binding they're blessing by saying, "Bennacht Time" (Blessing of Heaven).

The silence falls on the sounds of the forest, the birds and the wind in the trees are all stilled and for that moment time itself was stopped! Bodhmall vanishes through the Féth fíada.

In the silence, Muirne and Cumhaill sealed their union by joining foreheads and woad and as they lift to see each others eyes, Muirne says the words "Go deo Mo Grá" (forever my love) and Cumhaill replies "Mo Grá go deo" (my love forever).

***

FORBIDDEN TO BE TOGETHER

FOR THE RISK OF HIS LEADERSHIP

FOR THE SAKE OF HER BLOODLINE

FOR THE DESTINY OF A WARRIOR SON

IN SECRET THEY ARE BOUND

FOREVER

On that night during harvest in the time of Lughnasadh, under a The Great Hazel tree on a bed of the ancient Fern, surrounded by the last of the years 'Sceach Gheal' the last white Flowered Hawthorn, by the warmth of fire, they make love and lay together embraced beneath a clear twilight sky.

In her presence and by her blessing The Mórrígan walks around them and oversees. Prophecy and Legend passing soul from the otherworld to this world. She speaks the words of ancient time as Cumhaill and murine leave their physical beings and embraced they swim within the etheric space in time, losing all the heavy burdens of life and in that moment, they are love.

A joyful gaze on her face, The Mórrígan before she leaves.

The following morning, while Muirne sleeps, on his day of departure Cumhaill kneels and with his hands he digs near the roots of the Hazel and takes bread from his treasure bag.
He buries the bread as an offering.

He then, with palms of soil, recites the old Fianna prayer he learned as a boy.

The prayer is a sacred veil of magic used by The Tuatha dé to enshroud them from mortal men and protect them in battle or, in Cumhaill's case, a quest of danger.

Cumhaill says the words;

"éirím inniu le neart spéir, le gathanna na gréine, fórsa na gealaí, gile tine, luas an tsolais,

gaoth tapa, doimhneacht na farraige,cobhsaíocht an domhain, daingne na carraige".

"I ARISE TODAY WITH STRENGTH OF SKY,

WITH RAYS OF SUN,

FORCE OF MOON,

BRIGHTNESS OF FIRE,

SPEED OF LIGHT,

SWIFTNESS OF WIND,

DEPTH OF THE SEA,

STABILITY OF EARTH,

FIRMNESS OF ROCK".

He then kisses the forehead of his now sleeping wife Muirne and makes his way to the trade boats at Coriondi on the South East coast where he will travel as a fisherman to Brittania.

Chapter Two
~ Far and Away ~

On his arrival that afternoon at the harbor entrance, an old childhood friend and warrior of the Fianna, Liath Luachra, awaits by a trade ship with a smile and apple in her hand.

"Did you think I could let you go on this quest alone brother" she asked?
Cumhaill replies "no better company to watch my back woman" and smiles back.

As the ship sales out and the shores grow small with the sun going down behind, Cumhaill looks back and Liath says to him, "Sure we'll not be long and she'll be waiting for you".

Cumhaill ignores her and keeps looking back and replies, "Ní bhíonn tréan buan" (Strength is not enduring).
As the sun falls down behind the shimmering horizon Cumhaill turns to a disheartened Liath and asks, "Did you bring Fidchell "?

Liath replied with a smile "Tá eagla ar na Rómhánaigh roimh na Gaeil?" (Do Romans fear the Gael?).

They play the game of champions for hours as they make way on the week long journey across the Britannicus Oceanus. (Celtic Sea) and with Cumhaill now far and away from Ireland,

The Mac Morna clan see an opportunity to expand their reach across the land and make arrangements for Aedh to move up the ranks of The Fianna.

Unaware of the secret union between Muirne and Cumhaill, Aedh meets with the High Druid Tadg and asks for the official hand of his daughter Muirne.

Tadg gives him an ultimatum by saying, "When you take leadership of the Fianna, only then my blessing you will have".

Aedh looks confused by this request as he is well aware of the Fianna rules and to become leader it would mean he must defeat the leader in way of game or even battle, and unless Cumhaill steps down, Aedh knows that would never happen.

The pressure has always been o n Aedh to take leadership for his Clan as they believe it rightfully belongs to them and now that word is spreading about Cumhaill's love affair with Muirne without her father's consent, it is the perfect time to sway the King.

***

Three months have passed now since Cumhaill and Liath left home, and they finally sourced the location of the Spear of Victory.

After it was stolen during Beltane festival it was brought to Britannia Superior where the thief was killed during a roman raid on the city of Verulanium to prevent the ongoing barbarian uprising since the death of the great Celtic warrior woman Boudicca.

The artifacts from the raid were given as gifts to Roman generals and commanders and Romanized magistrates for their use in trades such as slavery and farming.

The spear somehow made its way from Britannia to the North West of Roman Gallia of Gaul outside the city of Augustodurum,where a slave trader lived.

The task ahead for liath and Cumhaill seemed to be a lot easier than they first imagined for such an item. The only explanation was that its powers were overlooked, which explained why it made its way to this place and not Rome itself.

Cumhaill was not sure the information they had been given by what he called a "Niggard", a miser and one for himself could be trusted. He was not convinced, but agreed it was worth investigating and paid him.

Without being noticed, and with Liath on look out, Cumhaill easily entered the grounds and retrieved the head of The Spear, broken from its Hazel wood shaft and kept in a box.
Into Cumhaill's treasure bag it went as they swiftly disappear into the night as if nothing had happened.

The next day, as they passed through a nearby village, they overheard the word that a traitor of Rome had been executed in the town square.

Liath went alone to see if it was true and it was, the head of a man on a spike, the same man who gave them the whereabouts of the spear in hope of favor and wealth from the local magistrate he informed.

The spike had a sign that said "PRODITOR" (traitor).

A light Roman cavalry galloped past Liath as she pulled over her hood and made her way back to Cumhaill.

The word was out now. Leaving Gallia with the Spear of Victorymay prove to be more difficult than retrieving it.

That evening they made their way to a forest shadow market for food and supplies for the trip home.

It was an illicit clandestine trade where you could purchase just about anything, weapons, snakes, exotic birds, animals, and the main attraction of slave girls. This was a place of evil frequently visited by the darkest of characters from all over the Roman Empire, it did not include Ireland.

Gaelic Ireland was untouched by Rome as it was said they feared our pagan gods and our ways, our culture and treacherous climate.

Cumhaill did not like the place and wasn't his confident self there.

They sat at a stall for food and to take a short rest. A moment passed and Cumhaill heard a familiar whispering voice around the forest to his left side saying his name.

He had heard this voice before. He recognized the voice as that of she, The Mórrígan.

Liath grabbed his wrist saying his name, "Cumhaill? Cumhaill? Do you not hear me? Are you unwell? Is it the food?".

Cumhaill replied, "I'm not myself, we must leave this place".

As they are about to get up, Liath sits back down and says "wait", as she looks over Cumhaill's right shoulder.

A small group of three Roman legionnaires just arrived to the trade. They were not looking for anyone to Liath and Cumhaill's relief; they seemed to be there for the slave girls only.

They laughed as they grabbed and pushed the girls like pieces of meat one by one.
Cumhaill heard the whispering voice calling his name again and at the same time he overheard one of the slave girls crying out, afterthe soldier had slapped her.

Cumhaill could not sit any longer and stood up, turned around and shouted in the Latin language he briefly learned as part of his Fianna training "SALVE! SOLUM RELINQUATIS EAM" (HELLO,LEAVE HER BE).

Liath tries to intervene, "Cumhaill, Níl" (No).

He gets the attention of the legionnaires as they laugh at each other and walk towards him and Liath. The haggling goes quiet for a moment of anticipation.

The Roman centurion who appears to be the leader steps up face to face with Cumhaill and says,"Quid negotii best tibi? Ava Scum"! (What business of yours? Celtic Scum!)
The Roman spits in Cumhaill's face.

Liath grips her sword.

Cumhaill doesn't even flinch and behind him, like a ghost, Mórrígan seemed to be controlling the situation and moving at the same time as Cumhaill slowly wipes the saliva from his face while moving his hand toward the knife attached to his upper shoulder blade under his hood and in one swipe, mirrored by Mórrígan but she closes her eyes.

Cumhaill cuts the throat of the centurion and in a flash, Liath thrusts her short sword blade through the lungs of the second soldier while breaking his neck.

The third soldier who took his time walking over cautiously, stepped backwards while looking for his sword, before turning and leaving the scene.

Cumhaill, placing his foot on the chest of the now kneeling and rapidly bleeding centurion, pushes him to the ground saying, "Na Fianna Éireann, Romanus laboursudatum!" (The Fianna of Ireland, Roman Scum!).

He then looks over toward the slave master and by sight alone puts the fear of gods into him. He walks toward the slave girl and cuts the rope with the bloody knife and sets her and the others free.

The slave master froze and said nothing as trade resumes business as if nothing happened.

The girl looked back at him with thankful eyes as she and the others leave and run for their lives.

Cumhaill and Liath know it won't be long before the third soldier gets back to town so they to leave and head to the point on the beach beyond the forest where a small fishing boat that Cumhaill purchased from a man that morning is there waiting for them.

They decide its best to wait until morning as an overcast night is upon them and it's no time to make sail. Also, the boat would not be there until the morrow so they sleep in the forest like many times before.

During the night a lucid dream awakes Cumhaill, it was his sister Bodhmall as a little girl crying after him as he left as a boy for his Fianna trials.

She sobbed and sobbed and called his name, asking him to come back and not to go. It was when her voice changed to an adult that it startled him awake.

It was nearly morning now and the sun was about to rise so he left Liath sleeping and walked to the beach to check if the boat was there.

The boat was not there and Cumhaill slowly fell to his knees, broken like never before. He was no longer the young warrior with great time.

He looked out at the golden sunrise bursting through a blue red skyline with tears in his eyes thinking of home beyond the Oceanus where his love and loved ones stay.

And then a sound of voices, Latin in the distance behind him. He moves fast and swift like his training thought him without breaking a twig beneath his feet and steadfastly he makes it back to Liath and wakes her by squeezing her arm.

A Roman Cavalry and scout party are in the forest looking for them.
As Liath and Cumhaill move and hide they are forced backinland away from the beach.

They can hear the soldiers talking and Cumhaill understands:

"We have searched all night" said the scout to the centurion. "Keep searching, they are here somewhere" he replied.

They run and hide in time as warriors of the Fianna do. They will never be found by these men of Rome but they must eventually get to the shore in hope the boat is now there.

They come back around to a dirt path behind the Roman horses,and Cumhaill says to Liath,

"Fand! Inseoidh an sciathán dubh dúinn cén uair" (Wait! Theblack wing will tell us when).

"Aruacht Dé,ní liom féin mo shaol, iompróidh mo mhála"(By the will of god. My life is not mine, carry the bag).

Liath is concerned by Cumhaill's behavior and takes The Treasure bag.

They wait and, just as Cumhaill said, a black winged bird flies in front of the horses chirping loudly so as to distract them .

Liath & Cumhaill cross behind without being noticed.

The Fenian warriors move with speed and with the keenest sight of Feige. Running and hiding among the trees they make their way on the other side of the peninsula back up towards the sea to the location of the boat.

As they see the opening to the cliff-banked beach ahead, Cumhaill, with his peripheral vision noticed a crossbowman dipping his arrow into poison and taking aim at Liath as she is about to jump. Cumhaill, while still running, moves into her line of sight, blocking the view and stopping the bowman for a second as he looks up and then aims again at Cumhaill.

As Liath leaps from the forest bank the crossbowman fires the fierce poisoned arrow which hits Cumhaill in the lower left side of his back as he continues to run a few more steps and jumps off the edge to the beach below.

The soldier shouts out "SUNT AUDIENT!" (THEY ARE HERE)

Cumhaill lands hard as he now feels the pain and looks to The Treasure bag on Liath's back as she runs ahead up the beach. He gets up from all fours leaving his blood underfoot.

The Roman cavalry are not far behind and have made their way to the beach behind them. The cavalry gallop and chase as if they were hunting game, while sounding a Lituus war trumpet.

Cumhaill struggles and begins to slow down as he sees Liath and the boat ahead. It brings him strength and some comfort knowing the old fisherman was true to his word.

The war party is now very close as a surprised Liath helps her injured and exhausted brother in arms Cumhaill into the boat and pushes it through the white water.

It's too late for the Roman cavalry.

Liath and Cumhaill make it out safely as the group of horsemen and foot soldiers trailing behind look out in furious anger at Liath as she rows with all her might.

The Roman Centurion takes out his Pompeii gladius sword and points it at the boat with no words. His facial expression was enough.

Liath looks back to them and the tree line of Gallia and then to Cumhaill; she now sees the blood. An arrow has run through the side of his leather armour.

She says nothing at all and continues to row as the weather changes, the moving dark clouds above show signs of heavy windand rain.

Chapter Three
~ Leaving Gallia ~

hree days pass and in a mountain cave on the eve of Samhain, when the veil between our world and the Otherworld is thin, the Draoi Bodhmall prays over a smoldering fire of smoke for the safe journey home for her brother and family friend Liath.

At the same time both sleeping Cumhaill and Bodhmall speak toeach other.

Cumhaill first:

"A ghrá. tabhair abhaile mé, tabhair abhaile dtí mo mháthair mé. Geallaim go bhfillfead. a ghrá, tabhair abhaile mé."
(Love bring me home, to my mother bring me home. I promise myreturn, my love bring me home.)

Then Bodhmall:

"Tar abhaile chatham a dheartháir lion, tá mórán le déanamh agat."
(Come home brother, you have much to do).

As the boat sways and the wind of the sea whips its small sail from side to side, a pale dying Cumhaill opens his eyes to feel the rain on his face. He speaks again:

"Braithim tú a Fhand, agus iarraim ort. a bhandia na farraige… Sinn a thabhairt abhaile go slán, agus nár imímid artíst." (Fand

I feel you, Goddess of the sea I ask you… Safe bring ushome never to leave again.)

Liath replies to him,"Tá sí ag éisteacht leat, a dheartháir lion. ach big do scíth go fóill anois Treoireoidh Bodhmall agus Fand abheile sinn." (She hears you brother, rest now… Bodhmall and Fand will see us home.)

Cumhaill closes his eyes again.

Bodhmall takes a handful of ashes and walks to the opening of the cave. In direction of their homestead and beyond the sea, she blows the ashes from the palm of her hand, calling the name of her niece Chara, daughter of Crimmall.

Cumhaill sees a vision of home, the rings of the roundhouse and crannog, with the clan baiscne banner flying.

He sees Chara and friend running past and hears Bodhmall's voice, "Chara", and again "Chara" she calls.

Chara also hears the voice of Bodhmall and stops running, turning around looking for the call.

As time slows once again, Bodhmall uses her magic to send Cumhaill a message, a foresight of what's to come through Chara.

Chara takes a deep breath and begins to dance, but not a dance she is accustomed to. This dance was different; this dance was to be her uncle's destiny ahead and the prophecy to come.

The young beautiful and graceful Chara danced around the homestead garden with expression and love, and with passion for life. She moved her arms like the gentle swan, and, light on her feet, she twisted and turned to the sound of the Gaelic rituals; the wisdom she could hear and feel through the sacred Sidhe she inherited.

She danced the journey that Cumhaill had before him, his future and his son the Greatest Warrior of them all would be the one to make change for the good of all.

Chara finished and came out f her transcendence that day to exhale and continue on her way.

The weather is changing to an eerie calm and Cumhaill feels strength of blood for a short time, enough to break the arrow which Liath helps him to remove.

The wound is infected and salt water can help him but without herbs and medicine it will spread to give him little chance to live. Again Liath says nothing and covers him with a shawl and gives him food and water left by the old Celt of Gaul. She then pulls up the olive green sail to reveal a golden sun and, as the South East wind took hold and pushed them toward home, the grey she sees in Cumhaill's eyes once again begin to close with a glimmer of a smile in his cheekbone high.

And from above in the Magh More (upper world) of Tír na nÓg the view of a small boat only a spec in the deep blue green Muír (Sea) makes its way home with blessing to sacred Éireann

***

The next day at the homestead of the Fianna, at the school full of mostly girls, except for one boy too young to start his trials with his older brothers and boys gone for the day.

Ethlinn wife of Tadg overlooks the children in the yard as they play and dance to sound of the Bodhrán drummed by the boy left behind and the wicker making chores and cleaning to be done.

Now with child, Muirne spends time as a teacher at the Fianna school to keep herself busy and away from the watchful eye of her father and clan Morna.

Muirne calls the children in for story time. "COME CHILDREN, COME, COME, STORY TIME" she calls.
Ethlinn rushes the children into the roundhouse including the usual two that never listen, Áine and Maeve. "Quickly you two always late" she says.

The children make a circle around the center wear Muirne stands with her staff over a bed of ash.

***

The Gaelic crannog or roundhouse is not just a house or building.
It's round design has a purpose, and for many reasons it ismuch more than a place of shelter.

If you were to look down upon it from the sky or the heavens you would get the idea, and if you were to layer it with themany other Gaelic designs such as the Celtic chess game of Fidchell on to The Féige Find (Fionn's window) known only to those who understand the ancient ways.

The Féige is a Travel Door or gateway to the other worlds, and provides penetration, acumen, keen sight and steadfast sharpness like The Mórrígan and the warriors under her watch.

It also represents and connects the five rings of Ogham and the divination of land to include the yearly calendar of trees overlooked by the divine powers of our Sun, Moon, gods and Goddesses.

***

Muirne with her staff inscribes five circles into the bed of ashes and at the same time barefooted bodhmall in her moss- covered cave many miles away does the same, opening a gateway of communication between them.

Then a line from Beith to Muin (North to South) and Ailm to hÚath (West to East).

The children look around hearing the far away voice of Bodhmall as she chants ancient patois.

Both Muirne and Bodhmall, at the same time, knelt, took a handful of ash and CLAPPED together, the first CLAP causing cloud of ash above the children's heads, the second CLAP and again the third filled the room above them with an ash cloud.

The Voice of Bodhmall gets loader and white line images startto appear around the space above as the children listen with wide eyed enthusiasm.

Bodhmall begins the ancient tale of The Tuatha dé Danann:

"They came to Éireann with pride and weapons and armour of gold that shimmered against the eastern sunrise. In wisdom they came in dark clouds of smoke appearing to our ancient land and in the West they plundered her chieftain men of bags.

The dark, uncivilized Formorian descendants known as the Fir Bolg.
They landed on the mountain of Conmaicne Rein in Connachta causing darkness and blocking out the sun for three nights and three days.
Only thirty years after the goblin hosts of Fir Bolg took our fertile land, A well-deserved and vanquished blow to the people of bags.

It was without distinction the Tuatha dé arrived to Éireann, and without ships their ruthless course of truth was not known. Beneath the sky of stars from heaven or earth we do not know and cast no justice after the sunset.
The fire and fighting at Mag Tired was a battle for kingship surrounding the people of bags The Tuatha dé filled with the force of abundance and pride."

As the children stared amazed and mesmerized by the sunlight-glowing dust from the ash now floating out the roundhouse entrance it was silence, not even a breath could be heard.

And then to the back of the house the clear and mature words from Ethlinn began:
"It was from the North they came, and in the place they came from had four cities.

Great Falias where they fought their battle for learning and shining Gorias and proud Finias and rich Murias that lay to the South.

In those cities they had four wise men to teach their young men skill and knowledge and perfect wisdom.

Senias in Murias, Aias the fair-haired poet in Finias, and Urias of the noble nature in Gorias.

Morias in Falias itself and they brought from this four cities their four treasures, The Stone of Virtue from Falias that they called The Lia Fail, The Stone of Destiny.
The sword of light from Gorias was known as Claíomh Solais. The Spear of Victory from Finias was known as Lugh's Sleá Bua and The Forth Treasure from Murias was The Cauldron of Plenty."

Muirne steps in and says, "A cauldron just like ours that no company ever went away from unsatisfied. So can anyone remember from yesterday how our home got its name?" "No? Remember Dagda? He was the chief and king of the Tuatha and he had three daughters, Banba, Ériu and Fodla.

They were worshiped by the people of our land and every three years took their turn to rule. And can anyone tell me who our home was named after?"

In her cave Bodhmall could still see the children as the last of the magic cloud fades away and sees Áine raising herhand with exited response: "Ériu" she calls out.

Muirne looks to Áine with a smile; "Well done Áine" she says,"and did you know your name comes from the goddess Áine,   also of the Tuatha dé?"

Suddenly the doorway light is blocked by the shadow of a man that startled Muirne and the children, it was the stand in captain of the Fianna, Aedh Mac Morna.

"Come children go now! Story-time is over, Muirne your father is home."
The children and Ethlinn leave at once.

"Father is home?" Muirne asked Aedh, "Yes" he replied as he stands in her way.

As she tries to leave he grabs her wrist and twists her arm. "Wait, I need to speak with you," he says.

Muirne pulls her arm away from hi m and steps back. "Father isnot home Aedh is he? What do you want?"

Aedh replies, "It was the only way I could speak with you, weare one you and I and we belong to each other".

"I belong to no man, nor do I belong to you Aedh Mac Morna,
You stay away from me, my father will hear of this."
Finished, she tries to push past him again but he steps in front of her with his face close up with a snipping grin.

"Your father? Your father approves of our union and I have already asked for your hand, we will sit together like Bile and Danu."

Muirne pushes him with both hands and says "You are no god, nor am I, It's fitting you choose the god of death, I will rulesomeday but I will never be yours".

Muirne pushes past him again, out through the doorway and he watches her walk away he shouts after her "He will never return, Rome will finish your mortal."

He then hangs his head in disappointment.

Muirne makes her way through the woods as she fixes her layersof clothing and continues to hide her growing child.

In her anger she speaks to herself, "Isteach sadoircheacht a thit tu a Aedh Mac Morna. Le hainm mo shi ns a bhai neann do chinniuint, Mo mhacsa amhAi n a scaoi lfi dhdo shnaidhm."

(In darkness you have fallen Aedh Mac Morna. In the name of my ancestors, your destiny belongs. Only my son can unbind the knot.)

Bodhmall overheard the argument between Muirne and Aedh.

She collects the dripping water from her cave walls and bringsit to the cave opening and, with a pinch three times, and fling of her wrist she summons a storm to come.

Muirne walks down to the standing stone to pray as the thunder roles in the skies above. It doesn't faze her as she places her hands on the Ogham scripture calling to the gods to bring her love home.

"Come home my love, come home".

Chapter Four
~ **Come Home My Love** ~

After four more days at sea Cumhaill and Liath are close to home and in the distance revealed by her morning sunlight. Cumhaill sees the coast of Éireann with her pastured olive and emerald green blanket of grass lifted by the brown copper and gold soil with protected grey and black foundation, floating solid and surrounded by a plentiful green blue sea.

The sight of home alone was enough to give him strength again, that feeling of safety as a young boy in his mother's arms.

They finally make it to a rocky beach cove. As Liath pulls in and ties the boat to shore a disoriented Cumhaill stumbles through the white water away from Liath on account of his blurry vision, He can barely see. He falls forward and spews blood while grabbing the sand and crawling out of the water inside the rocky cove. In pain he climbs to dry sand, focusing on the shine of his bracelet, remembering as he struggles to turn over on his back.

He looks to the clear sky and reaches out his hand, reaching for the memory of that day when she came from behind the standing stone with her smile and bracelet in hand.

As the vision fades his arm without the necessary energy to sustain a hold comes down and Cumhaill falls into blackness once more.

Liath comes to him and lifts his head, worrying for him but refusing to give up on him, saying "Nil" (No).

She drags and pulls him across the stretch of beach towards a cave in the cliff and stops halfway exhausted from the weight of Cumhaill and their soaked clothing. She falls twice to her knees with angry tears and her temper builds as she punches the sand with a scream to the heaven above.

Her spirits are lifted again as she pulls him the rest of the way and into the cave. Inside the cave, she gathers driftwood and dry leaves from the beach and flint from the treasure bag for a fire. Removing their wet clothes she holds him in her embrace with her hand on his forehead waiting for the warmth of fire.

As time passes Liath prepares to leave and, as the cold is released from his steam covered body, she covers Cumhaill with dry linen and puts her head to his, saying "Imeod ar feadh tamaill uait dheartháir liom agus fillfead arís le cabhair"

(I leave for short time brother with help I will return).
Liath leaves for help with the treasure bag in hand.

***

Many miles away near the Fianna homestead South East of the Sleeve Bloom mountains, as the storm from previous days comes to an end, and a rain-filled river gushes through the glen, Muirne is alone with linen in hand as she sits on hunkers at the large limestone valley as if all is calm and knowing the storm is over.

***

Meanwhile from the North, Bodhmall and her wolf Grá travel down toward home. It is many years since she left as a teen girl in protest against marriage and in search of her own path as a Draoi. She sent Fiachra the crow ahead that morning for a clear path.

Muirne looks up to the sky and sees a crow fly over and begins to sing her love song for Cumhaill, her son and the people of Éireann.

~ come home my love ~

my love my love, come home to meto me my love
come home,
my love my love, come home to me
my love, to me come home

my father he will learn to seehow much you
mean to me,
our son will show him who we are
the greatest of all he will be,

my love my love, come home to meto me my love
come home,

his honour will bring united kingstogether our
secret land,
so proud his mother my warrior's son
to éireann he'll give his hands,

my love my love, come home to meto me my love
come home,

in time of times of glory will pass
for the cross of iron will come,
when daughters and sons are long then found
cursed man of greed will be done,and the songs
of grá will be sung

my love my love, come home to meto me my love
come home,
my love my love, come home to me
my love to me come home

come home to me my love.

As Muirne sings the last verse of her song she is unaware of a dark figure in black armour lurking among the trees, watching her as he whistles the tune she sings in a slow darker tone.

And elsewhere Bodhmall arrives at the entrance of a ring fort and stops holding her stomach with hand a sharp pain she feels, holding herself up with her other hand on the stone doorway.

"Cad é an doircheacht so atá ar mo dheirfiúr?"
(What darkness is upon my sister?)
She speaks to herself andlooks into the core of her vision.

Fiachra lands on a branch near Aedh and with a caw, he alerts Muirne.

Aedh retreats backward and decides another time it willneed to be.

****

On the day before, it was a day of joy and happiness for young Chara and her new friend Enid. A young ambitious runaway from Munster looking for sanctuary and membership of the Fianna byway of Crimmal's daughter.

After spending some time together, young love is beginning to blossom and Chara is very impressed by his skills and ways of the wild for a boy who never trained.

They race through the forest and pretend to fight as he teaches her his hazel branch skills. He is confident and full of life, climbing and swinging on branches as Chara looks on shy and happy with coming of age feelings she never felt before.

Forgetting time she decides to stay with Enid in his shelter in the woods away from the family homestead and away from anyone, including her father Crimmal brother of Cumhaill who is stand in captain of Clan Baiscne and the Fianna.

That night in a small shelter after hours of chat and innocent courtship they lay separately when "BANG"! The door is forced open by two large warriors of the Fianna. They grab young Enid from where he lay as he struggles and tries to put up a fight. Chara shouts "Fág é, lig dó imeacht! (Leave him, let him go!).

One of the warriors with one swing hits Enid on the back of his head with a small blackthorn club, knocking him out as they drag him out by his arms with his feet trailing behind. The other warrior speaks back to Chara in a firm tone,"Téigh abhaile Chara" (Go home Chara).

The warriors take Enid to a forest opening known as Talamh Portaigh or Bog Land, where they bury him to his waist, leaving him alone with only a square shaped piece of oak and a hazel branch.

Enid had no idea but this initiation is his first test, his first trial of the Fianna. Crimmal was well aware of Enid's courtship with his daughter and only too happy to determine whether he was worthy to be a Fianna warrior, a late starter but nine years of learning and training lies ahead for the young Munster lad.

***

Chapter Five
~ **Goddess Airmid** ~

Mist arrives on the beaches of Brigantas and the cove where Cumhaill fights for his life.

Footprints appear in the sand with a fierce bright glowing light bursting the air from a transparent window of the travel door, from which Goddess Airmid appears, walking in her beautiful flowing gown with flowers of golden hair.

Goddess Airmid of The Tuatha dé Danann, Healer of warriors andmother of the sacred herbs she left growing for the children of Éireann.

Perceiving her presence, Cumhaill moves with eyes closed and speaks "M'uainse annoys tabitha ó tháinís fé mo dhéin"(My timeis now, you have come for me).

Airmid whispers from outside but Cumhaill hears clearly, "Ciúnas Cumhaill ní mór duit a boeit láidir" (Silence Cumhaill you must be strong).

Cumhaill barely makes out her glowing figure as Airmid enters the now cold, damp cave and kneels down to him, putting her hand over his eyes.

As she begins to speak they fade and leave the cave. Using her powers, she transports them to another place.

To a herbal bed of green and gold with colours of old surrounding them and with a language he hears but does not under-stand, she speaks again:

"Bain den anam so na pianta atA ag gabhAil do. imaigh anois arf eadh tamaill eile. Is ionann liomsa mo bhAs-sa agus a shaol. agus nuair a labharf ar ar Báll air. chif idh se.
(Release this soul from all his pain. Leave now for another time. My death I take his life to be, When spoken in time hewill see).

She stands and circles around him three times and again he hears ancient parlance he does not understand, suddenly feeling a power, a force in his hands lifting them to hold two spheres of light as he feels his muscles contract and the piezoelectric magical energy lifting his soul and his body off the ground.

A third sphere larger than the others growing white gold fire in the cage of his heart chakra, as he trembles Airmid tells him to breath"iononAl agus exhale" (Inhale and Exhale).

"Tarraing d'anAil, a shlAnaitheoir na hEireann. a lach na bhFiann, Beidh mAthair an Taoisaigh mar mhAthair ag do mac. Cuirfidh se cothromaiocht idir deithe agus na fir troda. (Breathe dear saviour of Eire, warrior of the Fianna. Chief's daughter will mother your son, balance he will bring to the Gods and Fighting Men).

Airmid kneels again and takes him into her arms as the force fades she looks up through the top of the trees into the sky, her eyes of hazel now glazed, and her tears fall as she closes them. The silver drop spills down her face and on to the poisonous wound of Cumhaill, with immediate effect, di- lutes from his skin. She places her hand over it and begins to stand and, as she lifts her hand away, it was clean with no mark left to stay.

Cumhaill was completely healed and no longer trembling and back into the cave she spoke to him again,"Imeod liom anois go dtiocfadh do dheirfiuracha, ach ta la eile de do shells caite." (I leave and go now for your sisters will come, For another day your time will be done)

Into the light Airmid leaves the cave through the mist covered sun low in the sky to silhouette as she is hugged by its rays.

Cumhaill opens his eyes and rises a new man with a new soul as if been given another life, an extension of time to finish what needs to be done. He steps outside the cave and sees the boat at the end of the cove and walks toward it. Among their trappings a wrapping of cloth he didn't recognize, and as he opened its gold twine to unwrap he revealed its handle.

A golden head and man shaped handle, thought to himself, as he touched the glimmering glaive glow upon its leaf shaped blade, could it be he wondered while knowing inside his heart that it is.

An Claidheamh Soluis (The Sword of Light).

A gift from the gods, forged in Gorias and brought to Irelandby Urias with his noble nature. A true honour to behold for Cumhaill, connected with the champions of old such as Nuada and Lugh and Cú Chulainn.

Now it returns to yield its power through Cumhaill Mac Trenmór for his unborn son.

****

Liath arrives at a village with cause in her eyes and takes a horse shouting "In aim na bhFiann, I bhfAbh ara fhillfead" (In the name of the Fianna, I will return favor).

The morning fog was still thick inland on the bog land border between Leinster and Munster where a banner of Clan Baiscne stands into the wet soil and a young man alone awakes in fear of why he his buried in a hole.

Eight of nine Warriors without Cumhaill stand, a third of a Fianna war band surround in a circle the young lad Enid. As a potential recruit he is about to receive his first of many trials after a long night in the cold without food.

They make sounds like wolves and call his name to heighten his fear and make him senseless.

Enid can barely see the warriors through the thick fog. He is afraid but prepares by grabbing the wood shield and hazel branch and waits for what may come.

The first of the warriors takes his spear and haulers fiercely throwing at the boy. Enid doesn't see it in time but it flies over the edge of his shield, closely missing the top of his head.

One by one, the second third and forth send out their spears, and one by one the boy parries it by blocking spear after spear at the same time.

And with his shield again, the fifth and sixth men throw their spears and again the boy parries both attempts with the sixth breaking his shield in half.

The seventh warrior standing left of Crimmal, who goes by the name of Báll, is a big angry brute and doesn't joke or smile too often.

He grunts as he takes his spear and shouts up to the clouds with a "roar", before throwing his spear at Enid.

The spear like a bullet passed through the fog taking the hazel branch from Enid's grip. Báll is disgusted and storms off mumbling.

Crimmal laughs saying "Cad atá art a bháll, an buachaill róthapaidh duit ab ea?" (What's the matter Báll, the boy too quick for you eah?)

Báll replies "Mo mhallacht ar an mbuachaill agus ar bhain d'ádh leis inniu".
(Curse the boy and his luck today.)

Crimmal smiles at Báll until he turns with focus and looks to the ribbon on the spear of his absent brother stuck in the soil of were he would stand. He takes his own spear and takes a breath while closing his eyes as a breeze blows across the ribbon and Clan flag.

In silence the boy, ready with fear unlike the previous attempts, looks around grasping a broken piece of oak and feels the air touching his skin. His breath is heavy and it's the only sound he can hear now and looks out through the fog with a brave shout "NOCHT TÚ FÉIN!" (SHOW YOURSELF!)

Crimmal aims his spear up to the sky, leans backward his arm and just as he releases his throw a voice shouts out calling his name "CRIMMAL" he hears and the spear is away in flight and vanishes into the mist above.

Enid doesn't know why but he braces the shield with both hands above his head and Crimmal turns to see Liath on horseback at the opening of the forest. The spear pierces through Enid's shield pushing him on his back with the point reflection of his eye. He survives the final attempt.

Crimmal takes his brother's spear and walks toward Liath.

As the other warriors pick up the spears around Enid, they ignore him without speaking. Enid wonders why and what he's done wrong.

They walk away leaving him to climb out of the hole himself.

A warrior calls out "Teanaim a bhuachaill, tA an pas fiachra an gcead scrudu agat". (Come on boy, you have passed your first test.)

Enid's delight stays quietly in his heart.

"Crimmal looks to see?" (Where is he?), Liath replies (Brigantas shores.)

Liath with great concern "CA bhfui Liath replies" Cladaigh Brigantas".

"Cen doircheacht atA A choimeAd?" (What darkness holds him) he asked again and Liath replies, "Maireann se beo, ach nil morAn ama ann, Ni mor duinn ea thabhairt abhaile".
(He lives but time is little, we need to get him home.)

Crimmal turns and calls out to Báll before they leave to meet them at the shores of Brigantas with a horse carriage and send word to Tara that Cumhaill has returned.

Báll nods his head and they move fast and leave the Bog land, while Crimmal mounts his horse and with Liath they make haste and gallop away.

***

On the shores of Brigantas, unlike his usual way of wearing his sword on hip, Cumhaill puts The Claidheamh Soluis on his back with a shoulder strap showing the distinctive warrior handle uprightfor all to see.

He walks to the beach on the other side of the cove and sees a way up the jagged cliff side.

On his way up the hill he sees a small figure, it's a child, alittle girl alone. She seems to be waiting for him and stops to see her holding a hand full of dandelion and chickweed. She doesn't speak, she just smiles and hands him the goddess grain.

He takes them saying "go raibh maith agat".
She says nothing but a smile and runs away.

He looks at the flowers and then back to see if she looks back at him but she was gone out of sight, just like that, as if she had never been.

He tucked the flowers into his belt and as he picked some berries from the hillside for his walk home, a familiar voice once again in the air whispering his name and her vision he sees in the above as she moves with wind.

"Cumhaill Mac Trenmór" she whispers as a murder of crow arrive from the south like a welcome guard of honour, but he has a feeling he could not understand as if he was now under compliment or that he owed some sort of debt.

When he reaches the top of the hill he sees in the distance, Liath and Crimmal gallop towards him. He smiles and his mood changes to joy, Crimmal dismounts his horse leaving him with Liath and wraps his arms around his brother with a firm embrace.
"Is maith an rud é deartháir a fheiceáil duit" (It's good to see you brother). They embrace again and Crimmal paths Cumhaill's shoulder unaware of what's on his back as he holds him while walking toward Liath holding the Treasure Bag with The Sleá Bua of Lugh (Spear of Victory) safe inside.

She hands it to him and he, with his hand on her cheek, puts his head to hers saying "go raibh maith agat deirfiúr daor" (thank you dear sister).

She looks up at him with a smile saying "deartháir igcónaí" (always brother).

As they walk with the horses, Cumhaill looks around towards the sea once more and makes a promise to himself; never will he leave home again and with the golden glow from An Claidheamh Soluis (The Sword of Light) on his back, The three warriors like the children they once were head for home after yet another great adventure.

***

The winter is ahead as the Prophecy unfolds

Muirne is now with child
And Cumhaill must now tell his King

&

He must Confront Tadg mac Nudat

&

Tension continues to grow from Clan Morna as
Cumhaill's leadership is challenged

&

Upon the waves from Britannia revenge is coming

To be continued…

Illustrations

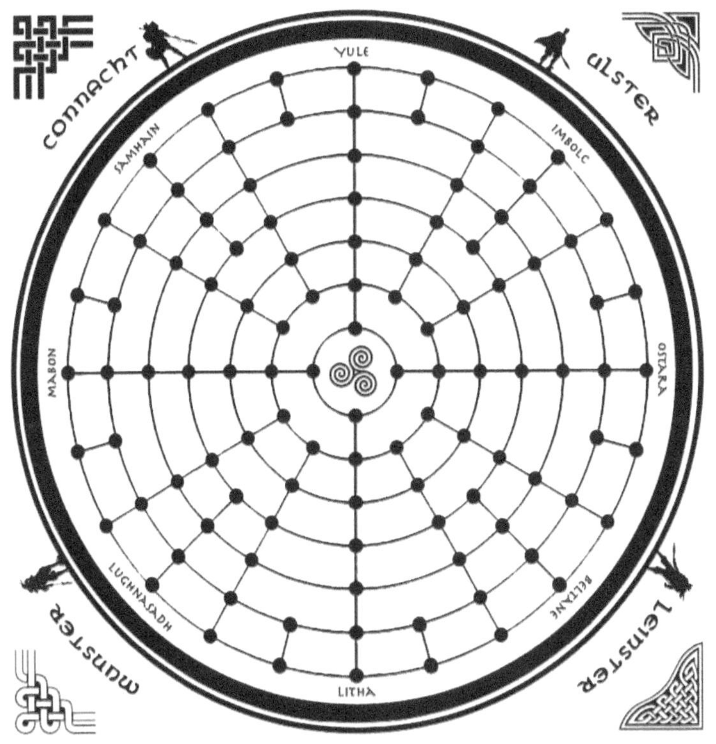

FIÒCHELL CLUICHE

CRANNOG
BHAILE
TUATHA GAEL
CÚ RAÐHARC
BIRCH
ELÐER
ROWAN
REEÐ
ASH
IVY
ALÐER
VINE
WILLOW
HAZEL
HAWTHORN
HOLLY
OAK

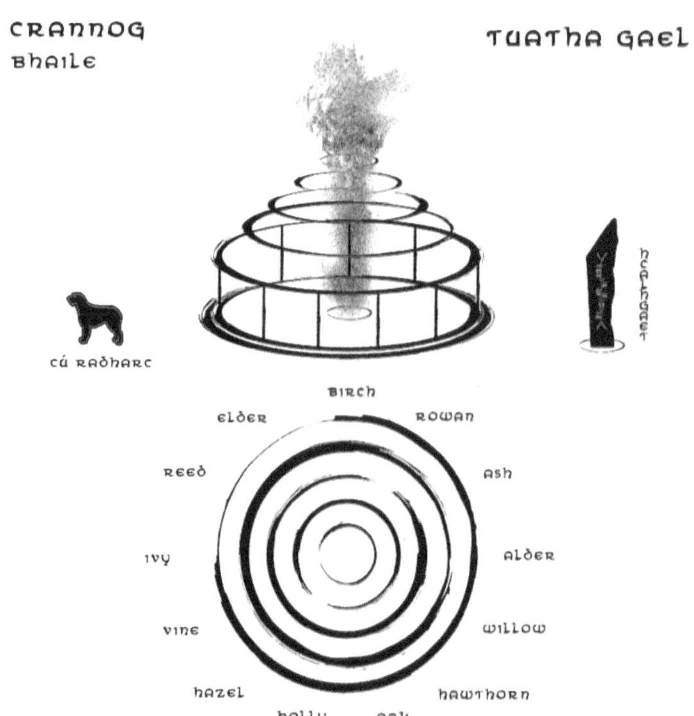

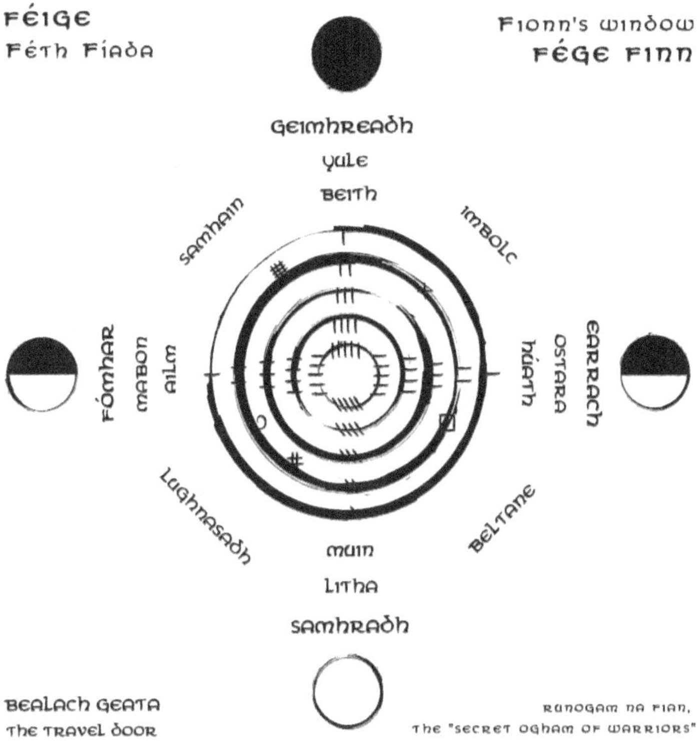

FÉIGE
Féth Fíada

Fionn's window
FÉGE FINN

GEIMhREADh
YULE
BEITh

SAMhAIN
IMBOLC

FÓMhAR
MABON
AILM
OSTARA
húATh
EARRACh

LUGhNASADh
BELTANE

MUIN
LIThA
SAMhRADh

BEALACh GEATA
ThE TRAVEL DOOR

RUNOGAM NA FIAN,
ThE "SECRET OGhAM OF WARRIORS"

DIVINATION
ÉRIU
MAGH MOR
DOMHAN LÁR
FAOIN DOMHAN
N
GORIAS
ULSTER
CLAÍOMH
SOLAIS
BRÚ NA BÓINNE
LIA FÁIL
UISNEACH
LUGH
SLEA BUA
CONNACHT
LEINSTER
FALIAS
FINIAS
COIRE AN
DAGHDHA
MUNSTER
MURIAS
S
W
E

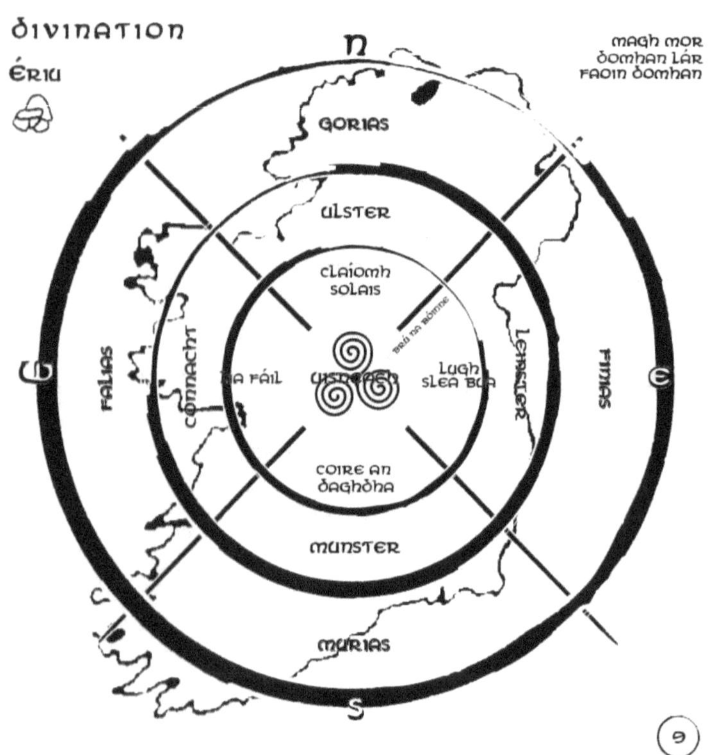

ANCIENT OGHAM
OGHMA
FILE GRÉINE

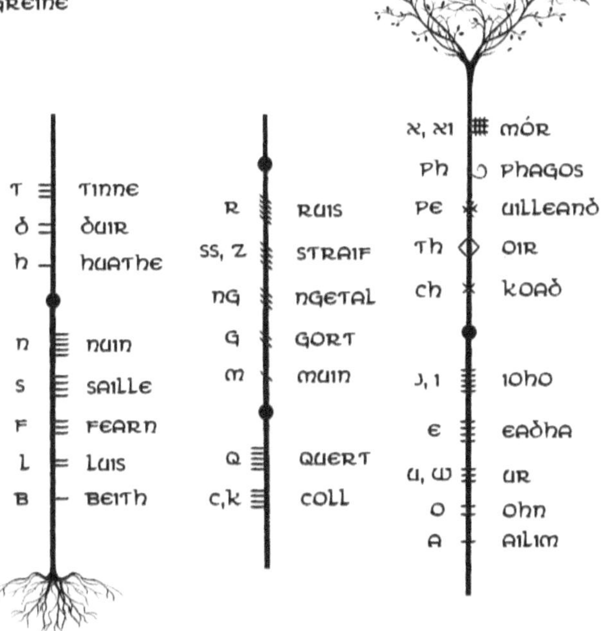

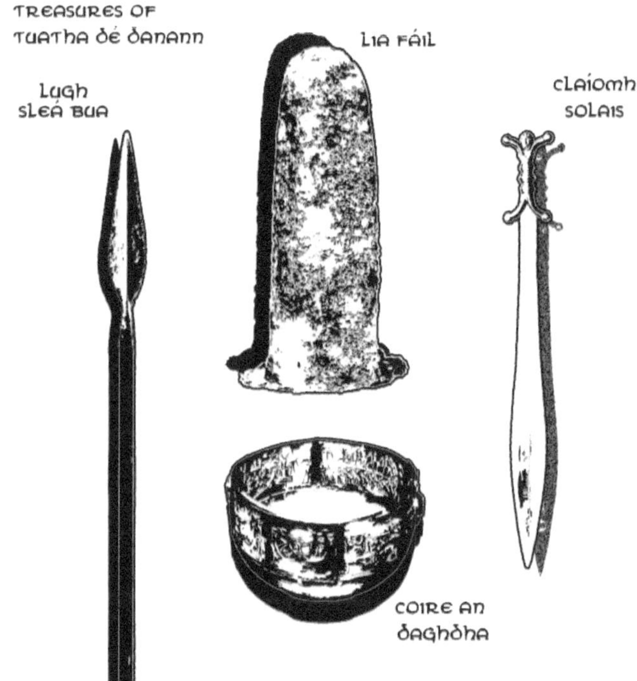

TREASURES OF
TUATHA DÉ DANANN
LUGH
SLEÁ BUA
LIA FÁIL
CLAÍOMH
SOLAIS
COIRE AN
DAGHDHA

TAÒG MAC NUAÒAT LEAVES BRÚ NA BÓINNE

BOÐhmALL BINÐING MUIRNE + CUMhAILL

Fianna homestead

Fianna Bodhrán Boy

STORY TIME WITH ETHLINN

ÁINE

muirnes sings come home my love

CHARA + ENID

CENTURION

LIATH + CUMHAILL

Goddess Airmid

Mórrígan

CELTIC ÉIRE
The abundant Land
200 A.D.
ROBOGDII
Cruithin
VENNICNII
grianán ailigh
Lamhain
Macha
DARINI Dunum
ERDINI
VOLUNTII
Regia
NAGNATE
Nagnata
Rathcroghan
Ehdani
Laherus
ÉRIU TEAMHAIR
UISNEACH
Maelicum
EBLANI
AUTEINI
Eheba
DOMNAINN
MENAPII
CONCANI
POLL na BRÓN
Regia Alterior
USDIAE
GANGANI
LUCENI
CORIONDI
Menapia
BRIGANTES
VELABRI
Iverus
IVERNI
eraunn
VODIAE
UTERNI
CELTIC SEA
oceanus britannicus
IMPERIUM ROMANUM

Written & illustrated by

JASON Ó FIONNÁIN